The Adventures of
Spike and Spe

Written and Illustrated by Nanny Bee
Edited by Jonathan Relf

How the Stories began.

For a few years I lived in a bungalow in Robertsbridge.

One lovely evening I looked out of the bedroom window
to see a family of Hedgehogs walking across the patio,
across the lawn towards the heather patch, then disappear.

A few weeks later the first story began while I was looking after
My two grand-daughters, Katy and Ellie.

Sixteen years later there are 12 stories to be published in books
containing two adventures in each.

I hope that children everywhere will enjoy the adventures
and friendships with Spike and Speedy.

Nanny Bee.

Third Adventure

Spike and Speedy's Springtime Walk

Today Spike and Speedy are enjoying an early evening stroll and a friendly chat about this and that. 'This' is the fresh air and 'that' being the large black rain cloud overhead.

"The air is lovely after all the rain," said Spike. "Yes," said Speedy, wishing Spike would stop looking around and hurry up.

He was hungry and had spotted lovely fresh greens along the path towards the park gate,

at the same time hoping to get there before the clouds burst. Of course,

this could be a good thing as it would mean he could have a shower while he ate his greens!

At last they reached the verge; the night was approaching, and the clouds had moved away.

While Speedy was climbing up the leaves, munching his way through dinner,

Spike was through the gate and on his way to the muddy bank of the pond.

He rushed towards it, making little squidgy noises as he stepped through the mud, eager to get to some food after his long winter hibernation.

"Are you ok?" shouted Speedy. "Yes, thank you" said Spike, with his mouth full.

"I was only asking because I'm sure I saw a cat walking through the gate just after you."

Spike shivered and looked all around him. There was nothing as far as he could see, but he still felt nervous. Although he was very spiky and was able to roll into a ball if necessary, he still had to be very careful.

The park was good for both of them, plenty of bugs and worms around.

Unfortunately, as he munched away, Spike became adventurous and his feet began to

sink into the mud.

He tried to pull a foot out, but as he did so, his other feet seemed to dig in even more.

"Oh, help me Speedy, "I'm sinking!" There was nothing Speedy could do to help, being so small.

He dragged some leaves over the mud to give Spike some grip and while he was

doing this, he spotted the cat with his paw out towards Spike.

Immediately, without thinking, Spike tried to roll into a ball.

Speedy had laid the last leaf over the mud next to Spike, and with a tap of
the cat's paw, he was able to roll into a ball to safety.

To their astonishment, the cat spoke to them, "Glad to be of help, dear friends".

Spike and Speedy could not believe their ears. A friendly cat!

"Thank you for giving me the push that saved me, what is your name?". said Spike

"My name is Sidney; I live on the other side of the park. "I saw you struggling

and thought I could help".

"You take care now, not all cats are as friendly as me. "Said Sidney.

With their tummies full and with feelings of relief, Spike and Speedy set off for home with happy hearts.

The End

Spike and Speedy's
Windy Day in the Garden

It had been a very windy day in the garden, the leaves were swirling around like dancers and trees were bending. By the time Speedy was awake, the wind had calmed down to a strong breeze.

As Speedy's eyes could reach above his shell, he popped them up to look and see

if there was any movement in the garden.

He was surprised to see Spike already up and very busy.

Spike was repairing the gaps the wind had made to his Heather House.

Speedy came out and started to help.

"Thank you, Speedy," said Spike, "please excuse me if I'm a little grumpy this evening!

The wind kept me awake all day."

"I'm looking forward to seeing what the wind has blown into the garden during the day, Spike.

Maybe we will find something useful."

One step ahead, he rushed towards the lawn and there, near the birdbath,

they saw lots of colours sparkling in the sun. This cheered Spike up very much.

"What are they?" asked Speedy, "they look like fairies!" but the moment one

settled next to him on the grass, Spike knew just what they were.

"Look Speedy, they're chocolate wrappers!" "Where did they come from, Spike?"

"Well, I would imagine someone had a birthday or a treat and didn't put their

rubbish in the bin!"

"That's not good," said Speedy, "Quick! Let's see if we can catch them before they fly away"

and as he spoke, a red wrapper landed on Spike.

They spent a pleasant evening chasing the pretty papers. It wasn't long before they had gathered a few each, so they hurried home to decide what to do with them.

Back home, they admired the wrappers. "Just look at these colours, Spike, they're beautiful."

There was a red one, a purple one, an orange one and one that was shiny silver.

Speedy was very keen on the green one, and he could see himself looking cool with it wrapped around his shell. Although Spike was not keen to wear any, he did agree that Speedy would look very nice.

Spike took the red and purple. The red, he thought would make a lovely curtain so that the sunshine or moonlight would shine all over his Heather House.

Making it feel warm and cosy.

By this time, it was getting near to daybreak, and they needed to eat, so placing the

wrappers safely at home, they wandered around the hedgerow eating whatever they could find.

Later Spike realised that Speedy was still wearing the green wrapper.

"Do you know Speedy, that looks so good on you, I might try it myself tomorrow.

"It's good we found these wrappers and could make use of them, they could have been very

harmful to other creatures." said Spike,

"Yes, we will recycle them when we are finished", said Speedy.

The End.

Printed by Amazon Italia Logistica S.r.l.
Torrazza Piemonte (TO), Italy

44428667R00018